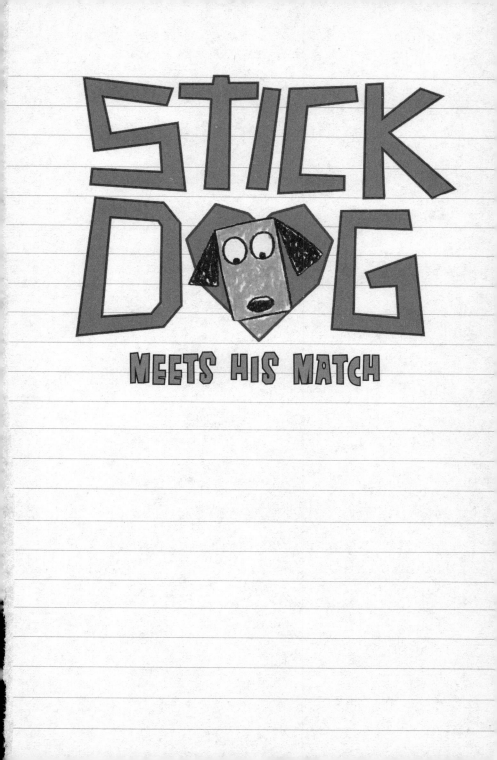

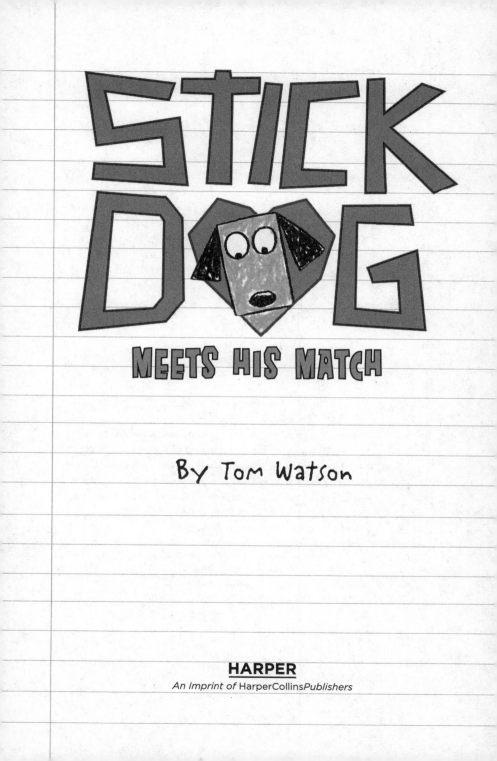

STICK DOG
MEETS HIS MATCH

By Tom Watson

HARPER
An Imprint of HarperCollinsPublishers

Library of Congress Control Number: 2019049250

ISBN 978-0-06-268520-9

20 21 22 23 24 PC/LSCH 10 9 8 7 6 5 4 3 2 1

❖

First Edition

Dedicated to Mary
(YMM)

TABLE OF CONTENTS

CHAPTER 1

SPRING HAS SPRUNG

When it was chilly, Mutt, Karen, Poo-Poo, and Stripes usually spent the night in Stick Dog's pipe. All five dogs would huddle close together, using their body heat to keep each other warm during cold, dark nights.

Last night was a cold, dark night.

But as Stick Dog opened his eyes and looked out his pipe, he thought maybe—just maybe—the day would bring some warmth. The morning sunshine looked strong and bright. He pushed himself up without disturbing his sleeping friends.

Stick Dog always got up first.

He looked at the others. Stripes, Karen,
and Poo-Poo were all pressed against Mutt
in some way. Mutt's fur was the thickest and
shaggiest by far. It made him the warmest.

Stick Dog made his way to the end of his
pipe and looked out at the little clearing
there before the woods started. He
closed his eyes and held his face up to
the sun, taking in the warmth for several
seconds. It felt good. He lowered his
head, opened his eyes, and gazed out at
the forest at the edge of that clearing.
He saw the first signs of life on the trees,

grass, bushes, and weeds.

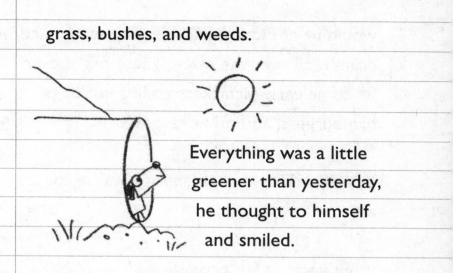

Everything was a little greener than yesterday, he thought to himself and smiled.

Spring was coming.

Stick Dog knew that meant good things for him and his friends.

The creek wouldn't be frozen over. They wouldn't have to break through the ice for a drink. Garbage cans would be smellier— meaning they could sniff them and determine what kind of scraps were inside without having to push the cans over. Small humans would be at Picasso Park, leaving snacks and crumbs all over the place. There might even be some early picnickers grilling hot dogs, hamburgers, and other tasty treats.

Yes, Stick Dog thought, spring was in the air.

It felt good. It felt promising.

But something else was in the air too.

Something that Stick Dog hadn't thought of.

Romance.

(Yikes.)

Chapter 2

A COFFEE QUEST?

When Mutt stirred and woke up, Stripes, Karen, and Poo-Poo woke up too. It had to happen that way. They were all sleeping against him. They yawned and stretched and rubbed their eyes. Then Karen hustled over to Stick Dog at the pipe opening.

Karen always woke up quickly—and with a burst of energy.

Stick Dog heard Karen's little dachshund paws patter toward him. He turned away from the calm morning and toward his frantic little friend.

"Good morning, Stick Dog!" Karen exclaimed, skidding to a stop against the dry metal floor of the pipe.

He smiled down at her.

"Do you know what I've noticed, Stick Dog?" she asked.

"What's that?"

"I've noticed that big humans often drink coffee in the morning," Karen said. This seemed like a very important observation to her. "It helps them get their day started. I've seen them drinking coffee in their cars in the morning. On park benches. Heck,

I've even seen big humans drinking coffee while they take their garbage cans out in the morning."

Do you mind if I interrupt here just for a second?

Thanks.

This whole coffee thing with grown-ups is, like, totally true. I know that for a fact because of my mom. She's not, you know, *normal* until she has coffee in the morning.

WITH COFFEE

WITHOUT COFFEE

Here's an example. Last Thursday, we ran out of coffee. That was not good.

Plus, it was the science fair, and I made a cycle-of-water diorama that I had to take to school. You know, evaporation, condensation, precipitation—that whole thing.

So Mom had to drive me to school.

That was also not good.

Here are a few of the things that happened on the, umm, trip to school. First, we sat in the driveway for, like, five minutes. I didn't want to make Mom feel bad, but finally I had to say, "Mom, you need to turn the car on."

Once we got going, everything was fine.

Until we got to the first stop sign on Armitage Avenue.

Mom stopped the car.

After about forty-five seconds, I said, "Mom, you can go now."

She kept staring at the red stop sign. She whispered, "But it says 'Stop.'"

"That means just stop for a few seconds," I said. It took a lot of work not to laugh. "You can go now."

Then she shook her head twice real fast.

Then she drove me to school.

Only it wasn't school.

It was the grocery store.

She put the car in park, looked at me, and said, "Good luck at the science fair!"

I figured it was probably best just to get out and walk the rest of the way to school. It wasn't too far. And my cycle-of-water diorama wasn't heavy or anything. It was just awkward.

So anyway, Karen is right. Grown-ups need to have coffee.

Stick Dog asked, "Why do you think big humans need coffee so much?"

"Because coffee is the best, Stick Dog!"

COFFEE

Karen exclaimed. "The
absolute BEST! It gives
me energy. It wakes me
up. Why, I'd take a bath in
coffee if I could! I'd swim in coffee!
I wish the creek was made out of coffee!"

"How many times have you actually had
coffee?" Stick Dog asked.

"Just once—when we got those awesome
donuts," Karen said. "But it was a day to
remember, that's for sure."

"It certainly was," said Stick Dog. He loved
Karen's instant enthusiasm in the morning.
Her joy gave him an idea. "You know what,
Karen?"

"What?"

"You know how we always go on searches for food?"

"Yes."

"Maybe before that we should go on a search for something to drink this morning."

"Do you mean—" Karen said, and began to shiver and tremble with excitement. "Do you mean we can go on a quest for *coffee*?!"

Stick Dog smiled and nodded.

"Really?!" Karen screamed, and jumped higher than she had ever jumped before— almost six inches. "Really?!"

Stick Dog nodded again and said, "Really."

Chapter 3

UNICORNS AND FAIRY DUST

"Where are we going, Stick Dog?" asked Poo-Poo as he, Mutt, and Stripes jumped over a fallen maple tree branch.

"It's called the White House Café on Wild Atlantic Road," answered Stick Dog. "It's just

through the woods, not very far at all. I've seen tons of humans walking out of it with coffee. I've never really thought of looking for scraps there though. It's just a coffee place, I think."

"*Just* coffee?" Karen asked, and panted. Her legs were shorter than her friends'—and she churned them much faster to keep up with the group. Because of that, she had to take in some breath as she spoke. "There's no such . . . thing as . . . *just* coffee! Coffee is . . . scrumptious . . . and magical. It gives you . . . energy! It's sunshine . . . and unicorns . . . and lightning . . . and fairy dust . . . all mixed together!"

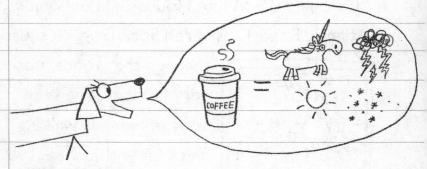

Stick Dog slowed and stopped then. They were at the edge of the woods—really close to the White House Café. His friends stopped with him. They gathered around

Karen as she caught her breath.

"None of us have ever had coffee, Karen,"
Stick Dog commented as he peered out
from behind a honeysuckle bush. He could
see the side of the coffee shop. There was a
concrete sidewalk, a bike rack, and an empty
garbage can there.

"Is coffee really sunshine?" asked Poo-Poo.

"And unicorns?" asked Stripes.

"And lightning and fairy dust?" asked Mutt.

Karen nodded her head,
grinned, and said, "All
mixed together."

"Shh," Stick Dog said, and

crouched down suddenly. "I hear some humans coming."

As they all watched, two women pushed two baby strollers on the sidewalk and approached the café. They parked the strollers near the bike rack, picked up two toddlers—a little girl and a little boy—from the strollers, and went inside the coffee shop.

"Okay," Stick Dog said quietly. "I think those two humans will come back out with coffee in a few minutes. We need a plan to get it from them."

"Don't worry, Stick Dog," Poo-Poo said. "I know just what to do."

"What's that?"

"Well, when those humans come back outside," Poo-Poo began. He seemed pretty confident in his plan. "They'll put those little humans back in the strollers. When they do, I'll charge out of the woods and bash my head into the garbage can as hard as I can. I am, as you know, one of the world's great head-bashers."

"Yes, I know."

"The humans will be so startled by the sound of my awesome head-bashing, that they'll turn to see what happened," Poo-Poo continued. His eyes widened as he detailed the next step in his coffee-snatching strategy. "While they look at the overturned can, you four rush in and push the strollers away as fast as you can! Once you're a safe distance away, I'll join you. Then we're practically done."

"Sounds like a great plan!" Karen exclaimed. "I dream of coffee sometimes! Coffee! Coffee! Coffee!"

Mutt and Stripes agreed that Poo-Poo's plan was absolutely terrific.

Stick Dog, however, did not.

"Poo-Poo, when you say 'practically done,'" he said, "what exactly do you mean?"

"I mean by that point we'll almost have the coffee," Poo-Poo explained. He seemed surprised that Stick Dog had trouble following along. "There's just one more obvious step to go."

"I guess it's not so clear to me," Stick Dog admitted. "What is that obvious step?"

"We write the two big humans a note," Poo-Poo said, squinting one eye and nodding his head at his own genius.

"Umm, what does the note say?" asked Stick Dog, not mentioning that none of them had ever written a note before.

"It says: 'Dear Big Humans. If you want your little humans back, then bring us your coffee. We will trade you.'"

Stick Dog was just about to explain that taking the little humans was not a very nice thing to do—not at all.

But he didn't need to explain anything.

At just that moment, the two big female humans came out of the café.

They each used one hand to hold hands with a little human—and the other hand to hold their cups of coffee.

Karen started to jump up and down.

Chapter 4

MUFFIE!

"What did you get?" asked the first woman as they walked toward the parked strollers.

"I had to get a decaf," the second woman said. "I had three cups this morning. I'm already pretty wired. What about you?"

DECAF →

"My usual," the first woman answered. "An extra-large, caramel-mocha, no-whip latte with three extra shots of espresso."

EXTRA-LARGE CARAMEL-MOCHA NO-WHIP LATTE THREE EXTRA ESPRESSO SHOTS

The two women put their coffee cups down on the sidewalk. They needed both hands to lift their toddlers into the strollers.

"Time for some head-bashing!" Poo-Poo scream-whispered.

He leaped over a broken branch at the edge of the woods.

But Stick Dog stopped him.

"No, Poo-Poo!" he said, and held him back.

"Why not?!" Poo-Poo pleaded. "The coffee is right there for the taking. We don't even have to run away with the little humans and negotiate their release!"

"They'll see us," Stick Dog said quickly. "They could call the police—or the dog catcher. We can't risk it."

"Then what are we going to do?!" Karen asked frantically. "I can see that coffee! It's right there waiting for me! It's a delicious, magical coffee fantasy! But if I can't get it, my delicious, magical coffee fantasy will turn into a malicious, despicable coffee nightmare!"

Stick Dog didn't know what to say—or what to do. Everything had happened so fast, he hadn't even had a chance to think up a plan.

But right then, someone spoke who made everything a lot easier.

It wasn't Karen.

Or Stick Dog.

Or Mutt, Stripes, or Poo-Poo.

It wasn't the first woman.

Or the second woman.

It wasn't the little male human.

It was the little female human.

"Muffie!" she screamed, and began to wriggle in her mother's arms, resisting the attempt to put her down into the stroller. "Muffie! Muffie!!"

"You want a muffin now?" her mother

asked. "But I asked you inside, and you said you didn't."

"Muffie! Muffie!! Muffie!!!" she yelled.

This yelling affected the other toddler quite quickly. He had apparently decided that he wanted a muffin too.

He screamed, "Muffie! Muffie!! Muffie!!!"

"Oh, for goodness' sake," the second woman said. "You too?"

As Stick Dog and his friends watched, the

two big humans put the two little humans back down on the sidewalk. They turned and headed back into the café. You could tell the big humans were in a hurry—a big hurry—to get some muffins for the little humans. They wanted them to settle down.

They didn't even pick up their coffees from the sidewalk.

Stick Dog said just one thing. He said it loud. He said it clear. "Let's go!"

They scampered out of the woods toward

the side of the café.

Stick Dog grabbed one of the coffees in his mouth, turning his head a bit to the side so it wouldn't spill. He realized pretty quickly that the coffee was safe and secure inside. The plastic lid fit tightly. Not one drop of coffee came out.

Karen was at the second cup. She was too small to fit her mouth around that coffee cup as Stick Dog had done. She looked at him with pleading eyes.

"Stick Dog!" she whimpered. "I can't do it. My mouth's not big enough!"

"It's okay, Karen," Stick Dog said calmly after setting his cup down carefully on the sidewalk. He smiled at her. They didn't have much time, but they did have some. He figured it would take the humans a couple of minutes to buy their muffins and come back. "Mutt, Poo-Poo, or Stripes can carry it for us."

Karen breathed a happy sigh of relief.

Mutt carried the second cup. Stick Dog carried the first. And they hurried back into the woods. In less than a minute, they found a little clearing among some oak

and maple trees. They set the coffee cups down.

Stick Dog was about to make a decision.

It was a decision that would affect Karen.

A lot.

Chapter 5

HOP! DROP! FLOP! STOP!

They settled down comfortably in that
clearing. The morning sun warmed their fur.
It took some effort to get the lids off the
cups without spilling a lot of coffee—but
they eventually figured it out. Mutt laid on
his belly and held the coffee cups between
his front paws, while Stick Dog gently pried

the lids loose. Hardly any coffee spilled at all.

It was then that Stick Dog made a fateful
decision. It was something that would affect
the rest of their day—especially the rest of
Karen's day.

Stick Dog said, "Karen, this is a special
treat just for you. And you're such a coffee
fan. I think you should have one drink all to
yourself. Mutt, Poo-Poo, Stripes, and I will
share the other one."

They all agreed to this idea.

Karen began to lap
and slurp at one cup,
while Mutt, Stripes,
Poo-Poo, and Stick
Dog took turns drinking the other.

What nobody knew at the time was that Karen drank an extra-large, caramel-mocha, no-whip latte with three extra shots of espresso.

And the other four dogs drank a large decaf coffee.

Karen was done in less than two minutes. She was small enough to stick her head into the big cup and was able to lick every drop from the bottom. When she was done, she pulled her head from the cup.

"I am in heaven," Karen whispered as she sat back against a nearby tree trunk. She closed her eyes, grinned, and rubbed her little dachshund belly. "Pure heaven. Wasn't it wonderful? Don't you guys agree? Now that you've finally had a taste?"

Poo-Poo, Mutt, and Stripes just shrugged.

"It was okay, I guess," said Poo-Poo.

Mutt nodded.

Stripes added, "It was a little bitter, to be honest. But, you know, I was thirsty, so it was fine."

"What?!" Karen exclaimed, and opened her eyes. She didn't understand how her friends hadn't enjoyed her favorite drink in the whole world. "You mean it wasn't the most amazing thing you've ever tasted?"

They shrugged again.

"Maybe your coffee was different than ours,

Karen," Stick Dog said in an attempt to make her feel better. "Maybe you just like coffee more than we do. It's no big deal. We can all like things as much or as little as we want."

Mutt wanted to help her understand. He said, "I like to eat things that aren't food at all. I chew on Frisbees and water bottles and rope and mittens and gloves and pencils. Shoot, I'll eat just about anything."

Karen nodded her head. She understood.

Then she nodded some more.

And some more.

And some more.

Her nodding got faster.

And faster.

And faster.

Stick Dog was glad about that, but he was curious about why she continued to nod—and nod so fast.

"Karen?" he asked.

"Yes, Stick Dog," she answered quickly. She was still nodding.

"You can, umm, stop nodding your head now."

"I'm nodding my head?" She was still nodding.

"Yes. You are."

Karen squeezed her eyes shut. It looked like she was using all her concentration to stop her head.

She finally did.

"Stick Dog?"

"Yes, Karen?"

"I'm going to run into the woods now," she said. "I'll be right back."

And before Stick Dog could say another word, Karen was gone.

Mutt, Stripes, Poo-Poo, and Stick Dog
stared at the spot between a clump of
dandelions and a couple of pine tree saplings
where Karen had disappeared so suddenly.
The rapid rustling sound she'd made had
dissipated. She was pretty far away already.

"Wow," Stripes observed. "I have never
seen Karen move that fast. Like never ever."

"Me neither," Poo-Poo agreed.

"Maybe she's been working out," Mutt
suggested. "You know, doing some lunges,
push-ups, and squats. Or perhaps
she enrolled in a Zumba or Pilates
class. She could be
strengthening her core.
Maybe that's why she's
so much faster."

Stripes and Poo-Poo thought that might indeed explain Karen's increased speed.

But Stick Dog had a different idea.

"That's possible, I suppose," he said. "But I think it might have more to do with that coffee she just drank. I think coffee might make her, like, super-hyper or something. And she's already a bit on the, umm, energetic side to begin with. So when she gets more hyper, it's really noticeable."

"Maybe," Poo-Poo said doubtfully.

"Mutt?" Stick Dog asked.

"Yes, Stick Dog? What can I do for you?"

"I was just wondering," Stick Dog said,

and smiled. He loved how courteous Mutt always was. "How do you know so much about exercising?"

"Oh, I've spent a great deal of time behind the Protein Powerhouse Gym over on Elston Avenue," Mutt explained. "It's where tons of humans go to exercise. I've found a lot of good stuff to chew on in that parking lot. Headbands, water bottles, old towels, that kind of stuff."

As if to demonstrate, Mutt shook an old white headband from his fur and began to gnaw at it.

"Where do they exercise, Mutt?!" Karen

yelped as she burst through some brush and
skidded and stumbled to a stop.

"Karen!" Stick Dog exclaimed. "Where did
you come from?!"

"The woods, silly," Karen said quickly.
She hopped up and down as she spoke.
"Remember, I told you! I went for a quick
run. I saw a blue jay, three worms, two
ladybugs, and myself—in my reflection at
the creek!"

"You ran all the way to the creek in that
short time?" Stick Dog asked.

"I had to run! I just had to!"

"Why are you jumping up and down like that?" asked Stick Dog.

Karen looked down at her paws and at the ground. It was obvious that she didn't know she was jumping.

"I can't control it! I have to hop!" Karen exclaimed, and giggled. "I can't stop!"

"Karen—" Stick Dog tried to say. He was a little worried about her.

"Hey, everybody! Watch this!" Karen yelled to get all her friends' attention. She jumped up even higher several times, fell to her belly, rolled around, and then stood back up on her four legs. "Do you know what I just did?! Do you? Do you? Do you?!?"

"Umm, what did you just do?" asked Stick Dog.

"I hopped! And dropped! And flopped! And stopped!"

"Karen—" Stick Dog said.

"Before I hopped, dropped, flopped, and stopped, you were talking about exercising humans," Karen interrupted. She turned to Mutt and asked, "Where do they do that?"

Mutt answered, "At the Protein Powerhouse Gym."

"Mutt was telling us about how he finds lots of stuff to chew on there," Stick Dog said.

"Where is it?" asked Karen.

"It's on Elston Avenue," Mutt answered.

"I know where that is!" Karen exclaimed. That momentary calmness had disappeared. She started to tremble again. "Let's go!"

And then Karen was gone.

Chapter 6

KAREN FORGETS

"Where'd she go?" asked Stripes.

Stick Dog shook his head
and sighed.

"I'm pretty sure she's on her
way to the Protein Powerhouse Gym," he
answered. He already regretted that he had
helped Karen get coffee this morning. She
was beyond hyper. He was afraid she might
do something dangerous—like run into
traffic or get lost. "We better go there too.
I think we're going to have to keep an eye
on Karen for a while."

Mutt led the way. In a few minutes, they were at the far edge of a big parking lot, staring at one huge building.

"Here it is," Mutt said as they arrived.

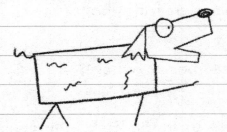

Stick Dog nodded, scouting out the surroundings. He always did that when he discovered a new place. It was his job to keep the group safe. They were situated behind a silver metal guardrail that encircled the whole lot. He looked at the large sign above the building's big glass doors.

It read, "Protein Powerhouse Gym—Work Your Body. Feed Your Body."

PROTEIN POWERHOUSE GYM

WORK YOUR BODY.
FEED YOUR BODY.

"Where do you think Karen is?" Poo-Poo asked, resting his chin on top of the guardrail and peering about.

"I don't see her anywhere," Stripes said.

"She might be in the back," Mutt said. "That's the safest place. There aren't any windows or anything in the back."

"Okay, let's go back there and—" Stick Dog said, and stopped.

He was interrupted.

He wasn't interrupted by Mutt.

Or Stripes.

Or Poo-Poo.

He was interrupted by Karen.

"Boy, am I glad to see you guys!" she
exclaimed as she scampered from the
parking lot and underneath the guardrail
to join them. "The funniest thing just
happened!"

"What was that?" Mutt asked.

"I couldn't remember why I came here,"
Karen answered, and chuckled a bit

at herself. "I mean, I knew it was my destination and everything. I wanted to come here. And I got here really fast! But when I got here, I had no idea *why* I was here! You know what I mean?! Crazy, right?"

"So what have you been doing?" Stick Dog asked.

"I've been running back and forth across the parking lot," Karen answered. "I saw all these cars. It just seemed like the right thing to do for some reason. What was I supposed to do? Sit around and wait for something to happen? I am a woman of action! I gotta move! I gotta be free! I gotta be me!"

"Makes sense," Poo-Poo observed.

"Sure does," added Stripes.

Mutt agreed as well.

"No. No, it doesn't," Stick Dog said, and shook his head at his friends. There was no anger in his voice at all, but there was concern. He didn't want any of them to believe that running in a parking lot was a good idea. "What you were doing was dangerous, Karen. Any one of those cars could have pulled out at any time. You could have been really hurt. It's never a good idea to run near cars."

"I could get hurt?" Karen asked.

"Definitely," Stick Dog said. "You should
never—"

Then Stick Dog stopped.

"What's that?!" Poo-Poo screamed,
grabbing everyone's attention. He jerked
his head to the left. He lifted his nose. He
sniffed at the air.
"I've caught a scent."

That's when
everything
changed.

Chapter 7

MEAT-A-PALOOZA

"What is it, Poo-Poo?" asked Stripes. "What do you smell?"

Poo-Poo closed his eyes and gave a series of sniffs, snorts, and sniffles, trying to capture that scent in the air. He squeezed his eyes shut in concentration.

"It's getting closer," he whispered.

Stick Dog turned his head left and right. He had no doubt that Poo-Poo had caught the scent of something. He had the strongest sense of smell in the whole group. But he didn't see anything coming toward them at all—well, except for a small truck headed slowly to the back of the parking lot. It was too big to park in one of the spots closer to the Protein Powerhouse Gym.

"You guys," Stick Dog said quietly, and moved backward into some weeds and brush. "Scoot back here with me. I think that truck's going to park close by. I don't want us to be seen."

Mutt, Karen, and Stripes all followed Stick Dog's direction.

So did Poo-Poo. He was backing up but still sniffing the whole time.

"It's even closer," he whispered as they all got safely hidden away. "That smell is even stronger."

Stick Dog kept his eye on the truck. They were safe and well-hidden, but he wanted to watch it just the same. It parked right in front of them. There was a big human behind the wheel. He got out and went to the back of the truck. He wore a stained white apron. Stick Dog couldn't see him after a few seconds and turned his attention back to Poo-Poo.

"I've got it!" Poo-Poo announced. His eyes stretched open. "I know what it is!"

Stick Dog looked at Poo-Poo.

So did Karen.

And Mutt.

And Stripes.

A wide smile came to his face, a droplet of drool stretched down from the left corner of his mouth. He said, "It's meat. It's meat! It's meat!! It's meat!!!"

Now, the dogs had eaten numerous things before, but there was nothing better than a juicy, tasty, meaty dish.

"Is it hamburgers?!" asked Stripes.

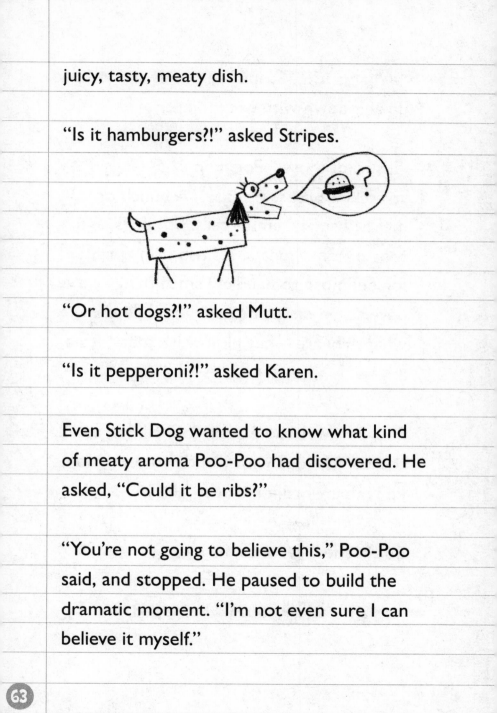

"Or hot dogs?!" asked Mutt.

"Is it pepperoni?!" asked Karen.

Even Stick Dog wanted to know what kind of meaty aroma Poo-Poo had discovered. He asked, "Could it be ribs?"

"You're not going to believe this," Poo-Poo said, and stopped. He paused to build the dramatic moment. "I'm not even sure I can believe it myself."

"What is it?!?" Stripes yelped as she hopped up and down with excitement.

"It's all of those," Poo-Poo said—a grin stretching across his face. "A bunch of meats! I smell hamburgers, hot dogs, and tons of other meats. It's too many meats for one nose to handle. I smell things we've never even tasted before! I don't know what they are—but I know it's meat! It's a, a, a—"

Poo-Poo was too elated, too flabbergasted, too confounded with wonder to even come up with a word for that smell.

But in a few seconds, he did.

"It's a Meat-a-Palooza!" he yelped.

MEAT-A-PALOOZA!

The dogs all lifted their noses in the air to find that smell too. And they all found it. Their heads swayed, their noses sniffed— and their mouths drooled.

"Where is it?!" Stripes asked urgently, and began to search all about the ground and under the weeds, grass, and brush. Apparently, she thought there would just be a pile of meat somewhere there. This immediately made Mutt, Poo-Poo, and Karen believe the same thing—and they began thrashing around looking for the meat too.

Stick Dog did not.

After a minute of this frantic searching,
Stripes came up with another idea.

"Maybe it's buried!" she screamed, and began
to scratch and dig vigorously at the dirt.
"It's a buried meat
treasure! Pirates
must have been here
hundreds of years
ago!"

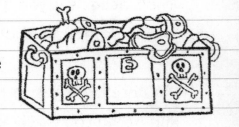

So, Mutt, Karen, and Poo-Poo started to
scratch and dig vigorously too.

Stick Dog did not.

"Poo-Poo?" he asked calmly as he watched
his friends. "May I ask you a question?"

"Okay. But make it quick," Poo-Poo said quickly. He didn't stop digging. "We're looking for a treasure chest filled with meat!"

Stick Dog did not ask his friends why in the world pirates would have been here. And he didn't ask why those pirates would bury a bunch of meat here—or anywhere for that matter. And he didn't ask if anybody really thought the meat would still be here after hundreds and hundreds of years. He had a different question.

"You said those meaty aromas were getting closer and closer, right?"

"Right," Poo-Poo answered, still pawing and scratching at the ground.

Stick Dog turned his head around. There was only one thing that got closer as Poo-Poo was smelling that meaty goodness in the air.

The truck.

Stick Dog snapped his head around to look at it. It had pulled in directly in front of them. He couldn't see the sides of the truck—or the back. He looked at his friends. They were digging like he'd never seen before. He decided to let them be— and stalked his way toward that truck.

He didn't have to move far to see what was on the side of that truck. There were a few big words. And then some smaller words under those. Stick Dog read the words:

"Mike's Magnificent Meats."

He couldn't believe what he saw. He read
the big words again to make certain—and
he read the smaller words this time too.
"Mike's Magnificent Meats. Get your meat
where the four streets meet."

He looked back at his friends. They were
still digging for a
treasure chest full
of meat. Then he
heard a metallic
creaking sound.

He snapped his head back toward the
truck. The back door swung open. Stick
Dog crouched down and scurried on his
belly several more feet to see what was
happening.

A big male human was at the back of the truck.

"That must be Mike," Stick Dog whispered.

The man had a two-wheeled trolley and stacked five boxes onto it.

Stick Dog stared at that stack of boxes and read the labels on their sides.

"Chicken, pork chops, hot dogs, hamburgers, steak."

And Stick Dog's stomach started to rumble.

Chapter 8

STICK DOG HAS A FEVER

Stick Dog watched as Mike, the meat man, closed and locked the back of the truck.

"I'll be right back, Lucy!" Mike called. He pushed the trolley across the parking lot and toward the Protein Powerhouse Gym.

"Who is Lucy?" Stick Dog asked himself. There was certainly nobody else around that he could see. Then his mind turned to far more urgent matters. "Could it possibly be true? Could that truck

LUCY?

be full of different, delicious meats? Could there be a place somewhere—a store or something—that is full of meat?!"

"What are you mumbling about over there?" Poo-Poo called from where he and the others were still digging.

"Yeah, Stick Dog," Karen yelled, and panted. She had been digging hard. Her hole was already very deep. "We're kind of busy over here. You know, trying to find that meaty pirate treasure. Maybe you should stop jibber-jabbering and get your tail over here and help out."

He said simply, "I found the meat."

Poo-Poo, Mutt, and Stripes snapped their heads toward Stick Dog. Karen popped

 out of the hole and
leaped toward him.
She was at his side
in three energetic,
joyful jumps. She
asked the burning question that all the
others were thinking too.

"You found the meat?!"

"Yes," Stick Dog answered, and smiled as
Mutt, Stripes, and Poo-Poo all came closer.
"I did."

"Where is it?!" screamed Stripes.

Stick Dog, still smiling, pointed toward the
truck and said, "There it is."

His four friends looked at the truck.

Then they looked back at Stick Dog. They didn't seem as enthusiastic as Stick Dog himself was.

"Oh, Stick Dog, Stick Dog," Stripes said, hanging her head and shaking it slowly back and forth as she spoke. "That's not a pirate's treasure chest. Not at all. It's a truck, Stick Dog. A truck."

"But the meat is—" Stick Dog started to explain. But he had to stop.

Poo-Poo had come even closer. He lifted his front left paw and patted Stick Dog's shoulder softly.

"It's okay, Stick Dog," Poo-Poo said gently.

"You just made a little mistake is all. You think a truck is a pirate's treasure chest. It probably happens all the time, old buddy. Don't feel bad. We all get a little confused sometimes."

"No, inside the truck is where—"

This time Mutt interrupted him.

"There, there, Stick Dog. Shh," Mutt said, and lifted a paw up to Stick Dog's forehead.

 "Be still now. I think you might be running a fever. Perhaps you're hallucinating. Maybe you're seeing things that aren't actually there. You think you see a pirate's treasure chest full of delicious meat, but that's not what it is. It's actually a truck, Stick Dog."

Karen rubbed up against Stick Dog's side to comfort him.

"Let's find a place for you to rest," she said quietly, and sort of nudged him a little to get him moving. "You'll feel better if you lie down."

Now, Stick Dog found all this amusing. But he also knew that Mike the meat man was likely coming back soon. And he wanted to get a good look at that truck before he did. Again, he figured the best way to do that was to announce it clearly—and quickly.

"The truck is full of meat!"

Stripes lifted her head and stopped shaking it.

Poo-Poo removed his paw from Stick Dog's shoulder.

Mutt took his paw off Stick Dog's forehead.

Karen stopped nudging him.

"It turns out, believe it or not, that the meat smells were not coming from a buried treasure chest at all," Stick Dog said. "They're coming from that truck."

"That seems unlikely," Stripes responded. "I mean, a pirate's chest makes more sense, don't you think?"

"Umm, well, I think—" Stick Dog said, and stopped. He had a feeling he wouldn't

need to do any more convincing. Thank
goodness.

That's because a soft breeze flowed across
the parking lot just then. It blew across the
truck and right toward the dogs. Poo-Poo
caught the scent again. He lifted his nose
in the air and began to follow it, stepping
slowly and dreamily toward the parking
lot. The others all followed closely behind.
Poo-Poo ducked under the guardrail and
continued the short journey to the truck.

"The meat is here," Poo-Poo said
triumphantly. "It's definitely in the truck."

"Way to go, Poo-Poo," Karen said.

"Way to find it, my man," Stripes added.

Mutt said, "Nice work."

And Stick Dog resisted the urge to slap his paw against his forehead.

Instead, he said, "You guys stay here for a second. I'm going to take a quick look around the truck."

"Stick Dog?" Karen asked before he started.

"Yes?"

"I really feel that urge to move again," she said. She hopped up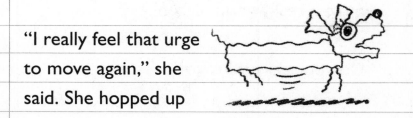

and down quickly. "I think I'm going to run around in the parking lot some more!"

"No!" Stick Dog said, stepping in front of her to block her way. "That's dangerous. Remember?"

"But I *have* to do something," Karen pleaded. "I need to move. Like now!"

"I tell you what," Stick Dog negotiated. He was worried about running out of time. He thought Mike the meat man could return any minute. "Why don't you go back to that hole and do some more digging? That will get you moving. It's a really nice hole. And you're a really good digger."

"Do you really think so?"

"I do," Stick Dog said. "For sure."

Karen dashed back to her hole. Stick Dog could hear her start scraping away at the dirt. He smiled and said to Mutt, Stripes, and Poo-Poo, "I'm going to circle the truck and investigate for a minute. I'll be right back."

He went along the side to the back. When he got there, he propped himself up and tested the strong metal latch on the door. It was closed securely—and locked. He wasn't getting into the truck that way. He went around to the other side.

MIKE'S
MAGNIFICENT
MEATS

The same writing was on this side of the truck. Stick Dog read it again.

"Mike's Magnificent Meats," he read out loud. "Get your meat where the four streets meet."

He paced past the driver's-side door, around the front of the truck, and back to the other side to join Stripes, Mutt, and Poo-Poo.

"Did you find a way in?" Poo-Poo asked urgently.

"Not yet," Stick Dog answered, and stretched up on his back paws, propping his front paws against the passenger-side door. The window was open a couple of inches on this side. He wondered if maybe—just maybe—he could reach a paw through that crack and unlock the door somehow. He rose up to look inside.

And he saw two things.

Two very different things.

The first thing made his heart pound. He knew they had to get out of there—fast.

The second thing made his heart feel funny.

Chapter 9

A FLUTTERING FEELING

When Stick Dog looked through that passenger-side window, he could see straight across through the driver's-side window too. And Mike the meat man was coming back. He was already halfway across the parking lot.

They had no time. They had to get out of there.

He dropped his eyes to look quickly into the truck. He hoped for a miracle. He

hoped there might be some meat on the
seat or something. Maybe he could shove
his front paw through the window crack and
reach it—and share it with his friends.

But there was no meat there.

There was, however, something else.

Well, not some*thing*
else.

Some*one* else.

And she looked up and
stared right at him.

And that's when his heart started to feel funny.

Stretched out on the long bench seat of that

truck was a dog.

A girl dog.

A German shepherd.

She had a length of yellow rope in her mouth.
She had a name tag on her collar. It said "Lucy."

Lucy tilted her head and stared up at Stick
Dog through the window.

He tilted his head and stared down at her
through the window.

He felt that funny
fluttering feeling in his
chest again.

And then Stick Dog got out of there.

Chapter 10

A DEEP PROBLEM

Once he was back on all fours on the
pavement, Stick Dog motioned quickly
toward the woods and yelped, "Come on!"

There was enough urgency in his voice
for the others to react immediately. They
hurried several feet into the woods and
stopped where Karen was still digging
her hole with tremendous energy and
enthusiasm. Only the tip
of Karen's tail stuck
out of the hole.
And dirt flew
everywhere.

Mutt, Poo-Poo, and Stripes hung their heads down into the hole to assess Karen's progress.

While they did that, Stick Dog turned his head over his shoulder to look back at the truck. There were plenty of branches, leaves, weeds, and stuff between him and the truck. He felt safely hidden.

He saw the truck vibrate as the engine started. He heard the truck *beep-beep-beep* as it backed slowly out of its parking spot. He saw it turn toward the street. He looked through the windshield and saw Mike the meat man behind the steering wheel.

And Stick Dog saw someone else through that windshield too.

He saw that female German shepherd.

Her paws were up on the dashboard. Her face was right next to the windshield glass. Her eyes were open wide and darting all around. She was looking for something.

Lucy's and Stick Dog's eyes met for an instant before the truck completed its turn and pulled slowly away, gaining speed as it moved across the parking lot and onto the street.

"Hey, Stick Dog!" Poo-Poo yelled. "We've got a problem over here! Over at Karen's hole!"

"On my way," Stick Dog called back. He was happy to be distracted from his own thoughts. He felt a little queasy—a little out of sorts or something. "Here I come."

As Stick Dog made his way back, he could see Poo-Poo, Mutt, and Stripes standing around the edge of the hole.

But he could not see Karen.

At all.

Karen was completely out of sight, still digging with incredible intensity and vigor. Clumps of dirt flew out of the hole in every possible direction. Stick Dog stepped between Poo-Poo and Mutt and looked down.

He saw Karen at the bottom of the hole.

He couldn't believe how deep it was.

"It was the coffee," he whispered to himself as he stared down at Karen digging frantically. In a louder voice, he said, "Karen?"

She kept digging.

"Karen," he called.

She kept digging.

"KAREN!" he yelled.

And Karen stopped digging.

"Yes, Stick Dog?" she called back, stretching her neck up to look out of the hole. "What's up? Please try to make it fast, will you? This hole isn't going to dig itself, you know!"

"I think you can, umm, stop digging now," Stick Dog said.

"I can?"

"You can."

"Why?"

"Well, it was just a way for you to get moving. You know, burn off a little energy. Remember?" Stick Dog explained. "Besides, we've got some work to do. We need to figure out where that meat truck went."

"Sounds good!" exclaimed Karen. "Let's go!"

Mutt, Poo-Poo, and Stripes all licked their lips. They liked the idea—and the prospects— of a meat-finding mission.

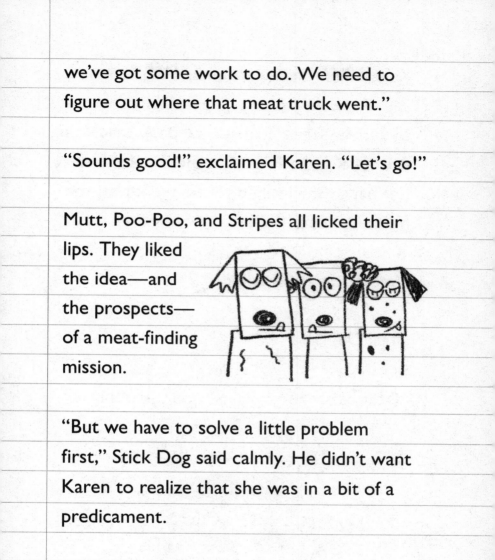

"But we have to solve a little problem first," Stick Dog said calmly. He didn't want Karen to realize that she was in a bit of a predicament.

"What's that?" Karen asked.

"Well, we need to get you out of that hole."

Karen then turned around slowly, examining the dirt walls surrounding her. She seemed to suddenly realize just how deep that hole was. She looked down at the dirt beneath her paws. She looked all the way up to the hole's opening.

"Stick Dog?" she called.

"Yes?"

"I'm a really good digger, don't you think?"

"I do," Stick Dog answered, nodded, and smiled. He was happy that Karen wasn't panicked. She was proud. "You're a really, really good digger. For sure."

"Stick Dog?"

"Yes?"

"Do you think it's as deep as the Grand Canyon?"

"I'm not sure," Stick Dog answered. "But it's pretty close."

Karen took a moment then and spun around slowly again, examining and admiring her handiwork. Then she looked back up at Stick Dog.

"Stick Dog?"

"Yes?"

"It's a great hole and everything," she called. "But I think it's time to go on that meat-finding mission I've heard so much about."

"I couldn't agree more," Stick Dog said, and paused for three seconds. "But first we need to get you out of that hole."

"Great idea," Karen called back. "One question though."

"Yes?"

"How are we going to do that?"

Before Stick Dog could answer, however,

Stripes spoke up. She had
a plan to get Karen out of
that deep hole.

And so did Poo-Poo.

And so did Mutt.

Chapter 11

THE CIRCUS PLAN

"I know how to get Karen out of that hole," Stripes declared with sheer confidence. "It's perfectly simple."

"How do we do it?" asked Stick Dog.

"We just go to the circus," Stripes responded. "Easy stuff."

"Umm, why do we go to the circus?" asked Stick Dog. He was kind enough not to mention that there had never been a circus around there. Ever.

"For the balloons, silly."

"The balloons?"

"Of course," Stripes replied. She seemed surprised that Stick Dog was not following along. "Circuses are loaded with balloons! They're everywhere. Red ones. Blue ones. Yellow ones. All kinds!"

"Umm," Stick Dog said, and paused for a few seconds. It looked like he was trying to figure out the best—and most polite—way to respond. "Why exactly do we need balloons?"

"It's totally obvious, Stick Dog."

"Can you, umm, just tell me anyway?"

"If you insist," Stripes replied, a little annoyed. "We get, like, three or four balloons. Then we tie the strings around Karen's belly. Then voilà! She just floats out of the hole. Easy-peasy, apple pie!"

"Great plan!" Karen yelled up her excited endorsement. "I love everything about it! The circus! The balloons! The floating! It's awesome!"

Poo-Poo and Mutt were equally excited.

"It's brilliant, Stripes!" Mutt exclaimed.

Poo-Poo added, "Totally!"

With everyone on board with her Karen-rescuing strategy, Stripes yelped, "Okay, then! Off we go to the circus! Follow me!"

Stripes, Mutt, and Poo-Poo took several quick steps away before Stick Dog stopped them.

"Wait!" he said loudly and clearly. There was not a hint of meanness or ridicule in his voice. "Wait, please!"

Poo-Poo, Mutt, and Stripes stopped.

"What is it, Stick Dog?" asked Poo-Poo. "Is something wrong?"

Now, Stick Dog could have answered that question in a number of ways. He could have said his friends had no idea where they were going. He could have said they had never seen a circus anywhere around there. He could have said it would take hundreds—maybe thousands—of balloons to lift Karen out of that hole. He could have said there must be an easier way.

But Stick Dog didn't say any of those things.

"I was just thinking," Stick Dog said instead. He cocked his head at an angle and raised one eyebrow. "I like this whole circus-and-balloon plan very much. I think it's clever and colorful and certainly well-meaning. But I have a problem with the *circus* part of the plan."

"What's the problem, Stick Dog?" asked Mutt.

"Well, circuses are great fun," Stick Dog explained. He uncocked his head and lowered his eyebrow. "There are rides and games and animals. Humans dressed in funny costumes. I mean, they're really, really exciting places."

"What's wrong with that, Stick Dog?"

"I just don't think we should go someplace that exciting without Karen," Stick Dog said. "I don't think it would be fair. She'd miss out on all the fun. It would be sad."

Mutt, Stripes, and Poo-Poo hung their heads. They realized instantly that they didn't want to go to the circus without their good friend Karen.

Then, suddenly, Stripes lifted her head. Something had popped into her mind.

"I know what to do, Stick Dog!" she screamed and jumped up and down three times. "I know how to solve the problem!"

Stick Dog asked, "How?"

"We take Karen with us, that's how!" Stripes exclaimed. "That way she won't miss out on any of the fun."

Mutt and Poo-Poo seemed to like this idea too. They nodded their heads up and down rapidly.

"We, umm, can't take Karen with us," Stick Dog said slowly.

"Why not, Stick Dog?" asked Mutt sincerely.

"She's, you know, stuck," he answered, and pointed toward the hole just to remind everyone.

"Oh, right," Stripes whispered.

"Come on, let's go back over there and see how she's doing," Stick Dog said.

They all went back to the edge of the hole and looked down at Karen.

"Hey, guys!" Karen said. She was excited to see them. "Are you back from the circus already? Did you see any elephants? Did you ride a Ferris wheel? I wish I could have come with you. I've always wanted to go to a circus. Just throw down the balloons, and I'll tie them around my belly!"

"Karen," Stick Dog said. He didn't think it was necessary to mention that they had

only been gone about a minute and a half. Instead, he explained, "We think it might be a good idea to come up with a different plan."

Karen shrugged her shoulders. "Okay."

"I think if I just—" Stick Dog said.

But he was interrupted.

"Don't worry," Poo-Poo said quickly. "I know just what to do."

Chapter 12

DROOL AND DROOL AND DROOL

Stick Dog really, really, really wanted to put some thinking into where that meat truck had gone—and to get Karen out of the hole. But he knew he would need to listen to Poo-Poo's Karen-rescuing strategy first.

He asked, "What's your plan, Poo-Poo?"

"It involves some very scientific thinking," Poo-Poo said slowly, trying his best to appear studious and smart. "I've been pondering this problem for a long, long time."

"How long, Poo-Poo?" asked Mutt.

"Days and days," Poo-Poo replied, and rubbed his chin with his right paw for several seconds. "Weeks even. The hardest problems often take a lengthy period of time to solve. And this one is a doozy, there's no doubt about that."

Stick Dog did not ask how Poo-Poo could have been thinking about Karen's dilemma for weeks when she had only been at the bottom of that hole for, you know, ten minutes or so.

Instead, he said, "It sounds like you've really put a lot of thought into a solution, Poo-Poo. What's involved?"

"It all goes back to the theory of gravity. You know, that time when a watermelon fell out of a tree and hit Abraham Lincoln on the head," Poo-Poo replied, nodding his head slowly. He then thought of other things that might be useful. "And we'll need Yo-Yo Ma's military strategy at Waterloo. And Neil Armstrong's inspiration in the Gettysburg Address."

Stick Dog almost laughed, but he lowered his head quickly and coughed instead.

Mutt observed, "I had no idea you knew about all that science stuff, Poo-Poo."

Stripes was impressed too. She added, "And history. I mean, wow, you know a lot about history."

"Oh, yeah. I know all about such things," Poo-Poo said, trying to be modest but not really succeeding. "There's Wilma Shakespeare's Theory of Evolution, for example. And there was that time way back in 2014 when Mahatma Gandhi attached a key to a kite string, flew it during a thunderstorm, and discovered the planet Jupiter. And then, of course, there's Harry Potter."

"Who's Harry Potter?" Karen called from the hole.

"He's only one of the greatest thinkers of his generation."

Despite his impatience, Stick Dog had to ask, "What did he do?"

"He invented the lightbulb," Poo-Poo answered confidently.

"I thought that was, umm, Thomas Edison," Stick Dog said.

"No, it was Harry Potter," Poo-Poo added even more confidently. He didn't like having his scientific knowledge and historical expertise questioned. "Thomas Edison was the first person to run a mile in less than four minutes."

"I see. Thanks for correcting me," Stick Dog said.

"I wasn't *correcting* you, Stick Dog," replied Poo-Poo. "That would be rude. It was more like I was *informing* you."

"Oh, umm, then thanks for informing me, I guess."

"You're welcome."

Truthfully, Stick Dog *could* have listened to this for much longer. It was great fun, but he needed to get things moving. He wanted to hunt down that meat truck. "So, Poo-Poo, how do we combine all of your knowledge about science and history to get Karen out of the hole?"

"We just all go to the edge of the hole, lean over, and then think of delicious food," Poo-Poo answered. "We'll all start to drool. I call it Poo-Poo's Scientific Theory of Drooling."

"But how does drooling get Karen out of the hole?" Stick Dog pressed politely.

"We don't just drool for a couple of minutes," Poo-Poo explained further. "Or even for a few hours. We drool into this hole for days and days. Eventually, the hole will fill up to the top. And then Karen will just float up! Simple!"

"Umm, Poo-Poo, I think—" Stick Dog started to say. But he was interrupted again.

"I know what you're going to say, Stick Dog," Poo-Poo said.

"I'm not sure you do."

"You're going to say that I'm a genius," said Poo-Poo. "You're going to say that my drooling-for-days strategy is the best thing you've ever heard. You're going to say that only one of the planet's great creative thinkers could have thought of this plan."

"You're exactly right," Stick Dog declared. "I *was* going to say that you're the only being on the planet who could come up with such an idea."

"Thank you," Poo-Poo said, and bowed for some reason. "Thank you very much."

"I don't think we can spend days drooling here though," Stick Dog said. He tried to put as much disappointment into his voice as he could.

"Why not?"

"I think we'll get super-hungry," Stick Dog said. "We won't eat for days. And we'll be thinking of delicious food the whole time. I mean, that would be awful."

Poo-Poo seemed to understand this logic. His tail drooped as he said, "But it seems like such a waste to not use such a brilliant plan."

"It is a waste," Stick Dog said kindly. "But it's not like we'll never ever use your plan. Next time one of us gets stuck in a hole, we can all think back to this day and say, 'Hey, remember Poo-Poo's great fill-up-a-hole-with-drool plan? Maybe we should do that!' That will be so nice, don't you think?"

Poo-Poo's tail stopped drooping—and started wagging. He felt better already.

That's when Mutt spoke up.

"Hey, Stick Dog?"

"Yes, Mutt?"

"I was just wondering if now might be a good time for me to share my plan?"

Chapter 13

SUPERSONIC JET THINGAMAJIG

"It seems to me we're thinking about this problem in the opposite way we should," Mutt began as he paced around the edge of the hole slowly. "You see, we've been trying to bring Karen *up and out* of the hole. I think we should turn that around."

"What do you mean?" asked Stick Dog.

"Instead of bringing her out of the top, we bring her out of the bottom," Mutt explained.

"We dig up to her from the other side."

Stick Dog asked, "The other side of what?"

"Well, the Earth, of course," Mutt answered simply. "Then Karen drops out. We don't need balloons or drool or anything! She just drops out!"

Poo-Poo said, "Sounds great!"

Stripes agreed.

And Karen yelled up out of the hole. "I'll start digging down right now! Then you guys dig up. And we'll meet!"

Brown clumps of dirt started to spray from the hole as Karen began to dig.

Stick Dog had to act quickly.

"Karen, stop digging!" he called, looking down the hole at Karen's frenzied activity. Some dirt hit him in the face when he did. He didn't want that hole—and Karen—to get any deeper. "It's a great plan, Mutt. And I'm glad everyone likes it. But there's no way we can go to the other side of the Earth. It would take years."

"What if we ran really fast?" Poo-Poo asked. "I'm a pretty good runner, you know."

"You are a good runner," Stick Dog said. "But it's thousands of miles."

Mutt asked, "What if we flew a great

big plane? You know, like one of those supersonic jet thingamajigs?"

"Yeah, Stick Dog," Stripes chimed in. She liked Mutt's idea. "Why don't we fly a supersonic jet thingamajig?"

"We don't have a supersonic jet, umm, thingamajig."

Poo-Poo asked, "We don't?"

"No," Stick Dog said.

Karen had been listening to all of this from the bottom of the hole and wanted

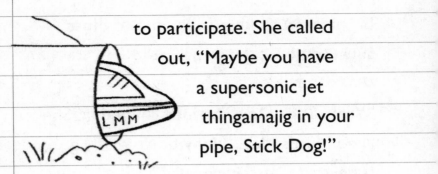

to participate. She called out, "Maybe you have a supersonic jet thingamajig in your pipe, Stick Dog!"

"I don't."

Stripes asked, "Are you sure?"

"Pretty sure."

"I think I know what happened," Poo-Poo said then. "Stick Dog, I bet you forgot where you parked your supersonic jet thingamajig!"

Stick Dog stopped responding then. He took a deep breath and looked down at the ground. There was a single dandelion there close to his left front paw. He took several calm, soothing breaths and stared at that dandelion. He watched it sway ever so slowly in the gentle spring breeze.

It swayed back and forth.

So slowly.

So calmly.

Back and forth.

So slowly.

So calmly.

Back and forth.

So slowly.

So calmly.

Poo-Poo whispered, "What do you guys think Stick Dog is doing?"

Mutt shrugged his shoulders. He had no idea.

But Stripes did.

"I know what he's doing," she whispered to Poo-Poo and Mutt. "I think he's trying to remember where he parked his supersonic jet thingamajig."

Stick Dog raised his head to look at Mutt, Stripes, and Poo-Poo. He had successfully relaxed.

"So?" Stripes asked when her and Stick

Dog's eyes met.

Stick Dog asked, "So what?"

"So did you remember where you parked your supersonic jet thingamajig?"

"No, I didn't. I don't—"

"So, what you're saying is," Poo-Poo interrupted. "You *have* a supersonic jet thingamajig, you just don't *remember* where you parked it."

"No, umm. No," Stick Dog said, resisting the urge to lower his head and look at that dandelion again. "And can we stop saying 'supersonic jet *thingamajig*'?"

Stripes asked, "Why?"

"Because you only say 'thingamajig' when you don't know the name of something," Stick Dog said. "But we do know the name of this thing. It's called a supersonic jet. It's big and fast and flies in the air. It's a supersonic jet. It's not a supersonic jet thingamajig."

"Stick Dog?" Stripes said, and squinted one eye. She was suspicious about something, you could tell. "You seem to know an awful lot about supersonic jet thingamajigs."

"No, it's just that—"

"I think maybe you're hiding something from us!" Stripes exclaimed. "You really *do* have a supersonic jet thingamajig, don't you?!"

Before Stick Dog could even answer, Poo-Poo exclaimed, "Do you really, Stick Dog!?"

"Where have you been hiding it?" Mutt asked. "In your pipe? Did you hide it underneath that old couch cushion that you sleep on? Is that where it is, you tricky devil? Did you hide the supersonic jet thingamajig under your couch cushion?!"

Stick Dog made a very important decision right then.

He decided he would not be frustrated anymore.

Or aggravated.

Or bothered.

Or exasperated.

Or annoyed.

He decided, instead, to be amused.

And he decided it might be easier just to play along with his friends.

"Okay, okay," Stick Dog said, and nodded his head and smiled broadly. "You guys got me. I thought I could fool you, but I can't. It's true. I *do* have a supersonic jet. And it's true I've been hiding it from you all these years."

"I knew it!" Stripes exclaimed.

"You can't fool us!" Poo-Poo added, equally delighted.

From down in the hole, Karen yelled, "Yes!"

"Where have you been hiding it, you sneaky fella?" Mutt asked.

"Umm," Stick Dog said, and thought quickly. "I hid it out at that big airport way down Highway 16. It's about fifty miles from here. You can go see it anytime. It's big and silver."

AT THE AIRPORT.

"You hid it at the airport?" Poo-Poo asked. "Well, how about that? Who in the world would ever think of looking for a supersonic jet thingamajig at an airport? That's just crazy!"

Everybody else thought it was crazy too.

"Yeah, you guys totally busted me this time," Stick Dog said, and smiled a little to himself. "But, unfortunately, since my supersonic jet is fifty miles down Highway 16, I think we better come up with a different way to get Karen out of the hole."

"How are we going to do that, Stick Dog?" called Karen.

"I happen to have an idea myself," Stick Dog replied.

Chapter 14

A MOST EXCELLENT HOLE

"I actually don't think this will be too
difficult," Stick Dog said to Stripes, Poo-
Poo, and Mutt. He spoke loud enough for
Karen to hear from the hole as well. "I
think if you guys hold my back paws, I can
lower myself down and press my front paws
against the bottom of the hole. Then Karen
can just climb up my back and out of the
hole. And then you guys can pull me up."

Poo-Poo, Mutt,
and Stripes
looked at him
dubiously. They
had their doubts.

Karen had some questions. She called up from the bottom of the hole, "Where's the style in that? Where's the thrill? Where's the panache?"

"Where's the drool?" asked Poo-Poo.

Stripes asked, "Where are the balloons?"

"Where's the world travel?" asked Mutt.

"I'm going in," Stick Dog said, figuring he had done enough explaining. He was ready to get Karen out of the hole—and find the meat truck with Lucy in it. "You guys grab my paws."

Thankfully, his friends did as Stick Dog instructed. As he got down on his belly and began to slowly lower himself down into

the hole, Poo-Poo and Mutt grabbed his
back paws. In several seconds, Stick Dog's
whole body was in the hole. He stretched
forward and planted his front paws firmly
into the dirt at the bottom.

"Hi, Stick Dog," Karen said upon his face-
first arrival.

"Hi," he answered, and grunted a bit.
It was a pretty uncomfortable position.
Uncomfortable—but not painful.

"What do you think of my hole?" Karen asked. "Pretty sweet, right?"

"It is, yes," Stick Dog replied. He could feel the blood rushing to his head a bit.

"You didn't even look around," Karen said, sounding disappointed. "How could you know how nice my hole is if you don't even look around?"

In this awkward position, it was quite difficult for Stick Dog to turn his head in any direction. But he did it anyway, scanning and surveying Karen's hole.

"It really *is* something," Stick Dog said after

wrenching his head around the best he could. "I love what you've done with the, umm, walls. And the dirt—well, it's just, umm, really nice dirt. Not too clumpy. Not too gritty. It's just right. It's a most excellent hole."

"Thanks, Stick Dog!" Karen exclaimed. "I'm very proud of it."

"You should be, for sure," Stick Dog said. Holding still in that position was getting harder as the seconds passed by. "Why don't you go ahead and climb up me now? You can grab my fur if you start to slip."

"Sounds good," Karen said.

But she didn't start to climb out.

"Karen?" Stick Dog asked. He couldn't really see her now, because his head was smashed sort of sideways into the ground. And his eyes were squeezed shut. His whole body was starting to hurt. "Are you going to climb out now?"

"Just a minute, Stick Dog," she replied simply. "I want to take a look around. You know, I really want to get a feel for the place. It took a lot of work to dig this magnificent hole, after all. I mean, I want to remember it years from now."

Stick Dog counted backward from ten silently. He wanted to concentrate his mind on something besides the blood rushing to his head, his totally uncomfortable position—and how he had to wait for Karen to get a "feel for the place."

While Stick Dog waited for Karen, the
others were having a very different
conversation up top.

"This doesn't
seem fair to me,"
Stripes said.

"Why's that?" Poo-Poo asked as he held
Stick Dog's back left paw. Mutt held the one
on the right.

"I don't have anything to hold on to, that's
why," said Stripes.

Mutt shot a quick
look at the thing
between Poo-Poo
and himself. He said, "Why don't you hold
on to Stick Dog's tail?"

"That's a great idea!" Stripes exclaimed. She was happy to participate in Karen's rescue.

Stripes reached down and grabbed the end of Stick Dog's tail. She squeezed and pulled on it.

"There's not much to grab here," Stripes said, noticing that her grip was already slipping. "You guys have his paw pads to hold. They're grippy. And you have his ankles as a place to hold. His tail doesn't have stuff like that."

"Maybe you shouldn't use your paws," Poo-Poo said.

"What should I use?"

"Try your mouth," Poo-Poo suggested.

"Your teeth should be able to get a pretty good grip."

"But won't biting down on Stick Dog's tail hurt him?" Mutt asked, showing concern.

"I don't think so. And let me tell you why," Poo-Poo replied. "When you get hurt—you know, step on a rock or something—your foot sends a signal to your head to tell you that it hurt."

Mutt and Stripes nodded, but you could kind of tell they weren't really following Poo-Poo's train of thought. He noticed this and explained further.

"So if you're biting down on his tail at the

end of his body," Poo-Poo continued, "I'm not even sure he's going to know it hurts. His head is way down in that hole. I mean, we can't even see it from here. I doubt very much that a bite on his tail will travel all that way to his brain."

"I'm not so sure about that," Mutt said.

Stripes seemed to be warming to the idea, but still appeared to have some doubts.

So, Poo-Poo added a little more encouragement.

"Besides," he said, "we have to look at the bigger picture here. This is an emergency rescue operation! I'm sure Stick Dog would agree that a bite on the tail is a small price to pay for rescuing our good buddy Karen."

Well, that was all the extra encouragement they needed.

Mutt nodded his head toward Stripes and then toward Stick Dog's tail.

And Stripes opened her mouth.

She leaned down.

And bit.

Hard.

That's what happened *outside* the hole.

At that exact moment, something else happened *inside* the hole.

Karen had finished observing and appreciating her hole and began her ascent up Stick Dog's body.

Right when Stripes bit down hard on Stick Dog's tail, Karen climbed onto Stick Dog's head. Her weight pushed his mouth together so that he couldn't yelp in pain as Stripes bit.

Up top, Poo-Poo said, "See, he didn't yell or anything. Not a sound."

Karen quickly scurried off Stick Dog's head, across his shoulder blades, and up his back. In less than two seconds, she was out of the hole. When Stripes saw her emerge, she let go of Stick Dog and hurried toward Karen.

So did Poo-Poo.

And so did Mutt.

They were so happy to see their friend.

And Stick Dog tumbled down into the hole.

Chapter 15

A TALKING TRUCK

Mutt, Stripes, and Poo-Poo all gathered around Karen. They patted and petted her as they welcomed her back.

"Hey," Karen said after a moment. "Where's Stick Dog?"

"Here I am," Stick Dog called from the rim of the hole. His head and front legs stuck out as he pulled himself up. While there was no way for Karen to do this—she was far too small—it was possible for Stick Dog.

"What are you doing in the hole, Stick Dog?" asked Mutt.

"Umm—" he replied as he worked himself out farther.

"Did you fall in, you clumsy guy?" Poo-Poo asked, and chortled.

Stick Dog didn't answer but scratched and clawed at the ground to extract himself some more.

"Only you, Stick Dog, only you," said Stripes. "After all that effort getting Karen out of that hole. And you go and fall in right after we rescue her? I mean, really?!"

Stick Dog's entire body hurt. His face
and head hurt from when Karen stomped
on it. His back and neck hurt from
being stretched out in such an awkward
position—and for such a long time. And his
tail definitely hurt.

He got all the way out, gave himself a little
shiver to shake the dirt off, and then looked
at his four friends. They were so happy to
all be together again. He decided not to
ask them about letting him tumble into the
hole—or about biting his tail. Instead, he
felt it was time to move on.

He said, "I think I know where that meat truck went."

Poo-Poo, Mutt, Karen, and Stripes gathered immediately around Stick Dog.

"We know that truck is full of different kinds of meats," Stick Dog said to his friends. He spoke quickly. They had a tendency, he knew, to interrupt him, and Stick Dog wanted to get this moving as fast as he could. "Poo-Poo smelled them all. And I read the words on the boxes that man took into the Protein Powerhouse Gym. And the side of the truck said so too."

"What do you mean 'the side of the truck *said* so'?" Poo-Poo interrupted.

"Yeah, Stick Dog," Stripes jumped in.

"Trucks can't talk. How could it *say* that it was full of meat?"

"I mean—" Stick Dog started to explain.

"Wait, wait," Karen interjected. "Is this some kind of magical talking truck, Stick Dog? I mean, if it can communicate, why don't we just ask it for some of its scrumptious meaty contents? We could just say, 'Hey, Mister Meat Truck, how about you share some meat with us'?"

"It's not just going to *give* us some meat if we ask, Karen," Poo-Poo said. "That would be ridiculous."

"Guys, I didn't mean the truck could actually—" Stick Dog tried to say. But his friends had placed their attention elsewhere now.

"Why not, Poo-Poo?" asked Mutt. "Why wouldn't the truck just give us some meat if we ask?"

"If you had a bunch of meat, would you just hand it out willy-nilly?" asked Poo-Poo rhetorically.

"No, I guess I wouldn't," Mutt replied.

"Guys, umm—"

"So, what should we do, Poo-Poo?" asked Stripes. "What should our approach be?"

"I think we should flatter this talking meat truck," Poo-Poo suggested.

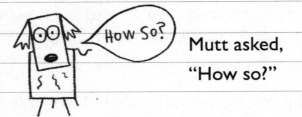

Mutt asked, "How so?"

"Well, we just give it tons of compliments and stuff," Poo-Poo explained. "You know, tell it how great it looks. How its tires are nice and round. How it smells good. How its headlights sparkle in the sunshine. That kind of stuff. Then, once it's feeling good about itself—and good about us—we could politely ask it for some meat. It would probably just spit some out the window at us. Then it's chow time!"

"Just a bit of flattery will do the trick?" asked Mutt. "Do you really think so?"

"I do," replied Poo-Poo. "You'd be surprised how far a few compliments can go."

"Great plan!" exclaimed Karen. "Boy oh boy. It's really fortunate that this meat truck can talk. I mean, who needs a plan when you can just ask it for stuff? That's the best!"

Poo-Poo was excited that his friends had bought into his idea so quickly. He said, "Come on!"

And with that, Poo-Poo took three quick steps away from Karen's hole and toward the parking lot.

Stripes, Mutt, and Karen followed him without hesitation.

Stick Dog did not.

"Stop," he called before they could go any farther. He didn't yell or scream. But he did raise his voice just a smidgeon.

They stopped.

"What is it, Stick Dog?" Stripes asked. "We're in a bit of a hurry here."

"I didn't mean the truck could talk," Stick Dog explained quickly. "I just read the words on the side. And it's also, you know, not there. It drove away a little while ago."

"It did?" asked Mutt.

"It did."

"Well, where in the world were we going then?" asked Poo-Poo.

"I'm not sure," Stick Dog said kindly. "But it doesn't really matter."

Stripes asked, "Why not?"

"Because I think I know where that meat truck went," Stick Dog replied, and watched as his friends turned around and came closer to him. "The side of the truck read, 'Mike's Magnificent Meats. Get your meat where

the four streets meet.' And there's only one place I can think of around here where four streets come together. It's right in the middle of town."

"So, let me get this straight," Poo-Poo said. He wasn't completely convinced. "You think if we go to the place where four streets meet, then we'll find the meat truck."

"And maybe even a meat store or something," Stick Dog said.

Then Stick Dog did something he doesn't usually do. He didn't wait to discuss the matter any further with his friends. Instead, he just took off toward town.

And, thankfully, Mutt, Poo-Poo, Karen, and Stripes took off right after him.

Stick Dog wanted to get to that place where the four streets meet.

He was thinking about the prospect of a meaty meal for his friends and himself.

And he was thinking about that German shepherd.

Chapter 16

DOG FOOD!

They got to the edge of town quickly. But when they got there, they moved much slower to get to its center. They didn't want to be spotted. They ducked behind mailboxes, garbage cans, and parked cars. They peeked out from behind stuff to make sure there weren't any humans around before moving again. Eventually they got to the place where the four streets meet. From behind a bench on the sidewalk, they spied everything around.

They saw a flower store, a cupcake shop, a post office, and several other places.

And they saw Mike's Magnificent Meats.

"There it is," Stick Dog said, and pointed.

It had a big glass window in front. And
through that window, they could see a great
variety of meats displayed. There were
hams, sausages, beef roasts, pork chops,
bacon, and plenty of other things too.

Karen whispered,
"Is this heaven?"

Stick Dog was just as thrilled as his friends. He had never seen so much meat in one place in his whole life. But he knew they couldn't remain in their current position. Even behind that bench, he felt too exposed. He wanted to sneak behind the back of Mike's Magnificent Meats. He wanted to find out if there was a back door.

He knew they couldn't move yet though.

And he knew they had to be silent.

That's because a woman walked by on the other side of the street just then. She had a dog walking beside her.

It was a beagle.

"Shh," whispered Stick Dog.

Now, he and his friends had often seen other dogs, of course. When they had, those other dogs always had humans with them—just like this beagle. And Stick Dog and his friends were strays. They always—*always*—stayed hidden the best they could when humans were around. Stick Dog never risked the chance that he or his friends might be caught and their group separated.

So they stayed hidden—and stayed quiet—behind that bench.

Until the woman and the beagle were out of sight.

Only then did Stick Dog speak to his friends.

"Okay, it's time to move," Stick Dog whispered to them. "I want to see if this store has a back—"

"Stick Dog?" Karen interrupted.

"Yes?"

"Why was that beagle walking next to that female human?"

"I think the beagle and that human live together," Stick Dog said. "They're roommates."

"Why wasn't he tied to her with a string?" Poo-Poo asked.

"I think those strings are called leashes,"
Stick Dog answered.

Mutt asked, "Why wasn't there a leash?"

"You're right," Stick Dog said quickly and
quietly. He wanted to move out of there and
get to the back of the store. "We usually see
humans and dogs connected with leashes.
But sometimes we don't. Sometimes, the
dog just walks beside the human like that
beagle."

"Why didn't that beagle run away?" Stripes
asked.

"He must, you know, like being roommates
with that human," Stick Dog answered.

"But what about running around wherever

you want?" Poo-Poo said. "And knocking over garbage cans? And seeing the stars at night? And hanging out with your friends whenever you want? Wouldn't you run away as fast as you could to do those things?"

"I see what you mean," Stick Dog said and smiled. "But dogs who have human roommates like the way their lives are too."

"How so?" asked Mutt.

"Well, they always have a warm place to sleep," Stick Dog explained. "They always have food to eat. They always—"

"Wait a minute, wait a minute," Karen said. "Are you saying that when you have a human roommate, you're never hungry?"

NEVER
HUNGRY?

"Pretty much," Stick Dog said. "I think humans feed their dog roommates every day."

"Every day?!" Poo-Poo exclaimed.

"Shh," Stick Dog said. He took a quick glance above the bench. He saw a male human coming toward them on their side of the street. He ducked back down. "There's a human coming toward us. But, yes, humans feed their dog roommates every day."

An unusual sentiment seemed to wash across his friends then as they considered this idea. Mutt, Karen, Poo-Poo, and Stripes

tilted their heads a little. They glanced
upward a bit.

Poo-Poo seemed to speak for the group
when he said quietly, "Getting fed every day
wouldn't be so bad. I mean, there are days
when we don't find anything to eat at all."

"It's true," Stick Dog said. "There are some
days when we don't eat."

"What do these human roommates feed
the dogs?" asked Mutt.

 "Do they feed them
hamburgers, hot
dogs, and pizza?" asked Stripes.

 Karen asked, "And ice cream,
donuts, and spaghetti?"

"And candy and barbecue ribs and tacos?" asked Poo-Poo.

"No, I don't think so," Stick Dog whispered even more quietly. He figured that male human was getting pretty close by now. "I don't think dogs with human roommates get things like that to eat at all. I think they get dog food."

"Dog food!" Poo-Poo exclaimed.

"Shh!"

"Food made out of dogs?!" Stripes yelped.

"Shh! Shh!" Stick Dog answered as quietly and urgently as he could. "Not food made *out of* dogs. Food made *for* dogs. It comes in little pieces."

"What's it made out of?"

"I'm not sure anybody really knows," Stick Dog whispered. He could hear the big male human's footsteps getting closer on the sidewalk. "They eat it every day though, I think. It's just given to them."

Then a completely different feeling seemed to come over his friends.

"I wouldn't want to do that!" Poo-Poo exclaimed, shaking his head. "Who would want to eat the same thing every day! And not even know what it is! That's

ridiculous! Where's the variety?! Where's the hunt? Where's the adventure?!"

Stripes, Mutt, and Karen all agreed with Poo-Poo.

"Quiet!" Stick Dog scream-whispered.

Those footsteps were super-close now.

And then they stopped.

And the male human sat down.

On the bench.

Chapter 17

SCOOTER TAKES A SEAT

"What a beautiful day," the man said as he plopped down on the bench. "I'm just going to sit and enjoy it for a minute."

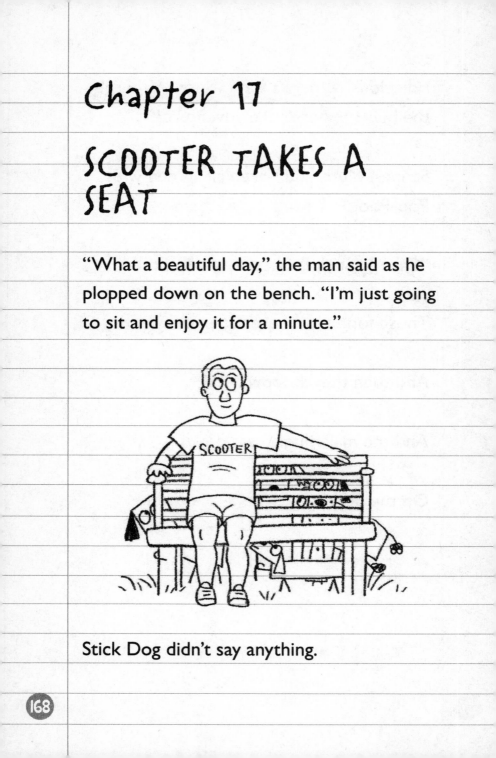

Stick Dog didn't say anything.

He couldn't.

Obviously.

That male human was just inches away.

Stick Dog held a paw up to his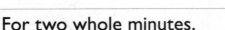
mouth and stared wide-eyed and
seriously at his friends. Thankfully,
they all understood. They didn't
make a sound or move a muscle.

For two whole minutes.

During that two minutes, the man stretched
and sighed. He stared up as the white clouds
drifted across the deep blue sky. He yawned
and stretched again. And then he stood up.

"Well, Scott," he said to himself. "These

supplies for the barbecue are not going to buy themselves. Time to get moving."

The man looked left, then right, then left again. He stepped off the sidewalk and onto the street.

He headed straight toward Mike's Magnificent Meats.

And Stick Dog got ready to go too.

Chapter 18

SNEAKY AND STEALTHY

The discussion he just had with his friends about that beagle made an idea pop into Stick Dog's head. It happened right when that human started toward Mike's Magnificent Meats.

Sometimes, Stick Dog reminded himself, dogs walk close to their human roommates without a leash.

It looks perfectly natural.

Nobody would suspect a thing.

Stick Dog snapped his head over his shoulder to look at his friends.

"I'm going into the meat store!" he said quickly and with complete conviction. "You guys sneak around to the back. I'll try to meet you there!"

Before any of his friends could say a word, Stick Dog hustled out from behind the bench. He looked left. He looked right. He saw a few humans around, but none of them were very close. There were no cars coming.

He looked ahead.

Scott, the human, was almost halfway across the street.

And Stick Dog hurried to follow him.

He was used to moving quietly— and sneakily.

He had snuck around town looking for scraps. He had moved through the woods silently to avoid detection when he could hear humans wandering about. He wasn't absolutely positive he could move behind the male human without being seen by him.

But he thought he had a pretty good chance.

Stick Dog took his steps in rhythm with the man's steps. He set his paw pads down lightly without making a sound or scattering a pebble. He crouched his head down, lowering his profile. They crossed the double-yellow line in the middle of the street and kept going.

Stick Dog stayed stealthy.

The man stepped onto the sidewalk—and two seconds later, so did Stick Dog.

The man pulled the glass door open.

Stick Dog could see Mike the meat man past the counter inside the store. He was turned away from the door, cutting something with a big rectangular knife at a table in the back.

Scott went into the store.

So did Stick Dog.

Chapter 19

STICK DOG IS STUCK

Inside the store, there were two long glass cases where the vast variety of meats were displayed. Those two cases were connected by a counter with a cash register straight ahead. There was a door in the back of the store near where Mike, the meat man was. As Scott headed toward the counter, Stick Dog turned left as quietly as he could.

He crouched low behind the long glass case. He propped himself up just high enough to see the humans in the store. He could hear them too.

"Scott, good to see you," Mike the meat man said as he turned around and put his metal cleaver down. "Is it a barbecue weekend?"

"Yes, it is, Mike," Scott said, smiling and looking around.

Stick Dog ducked down. As he did, he saw—and smelled—what was in the glass case he hid behind. There were platters of big hamburger patties, huge piles of sausages, and a bunch of the longest hot dogs he'd ever seen.

He listened to the conversation between the two humans.

"Well, what will it be? I just cut some rib eye steaks," Mike the meat man asked, walking over to the other glass case. He pointed at the steaks from behind the case while Scott eyeballed them from the front. "They're good for grilling."

"Sounds great, but I think I'll go with the basics this time," Scott answered after thinking about it for a moment. "Alex likes hamburgers and Josh likes hot dogs. Do you have any foot-long hot dogs?"

Stick Dog opened his eyes wide.

Hamburgers and hot dogs? That's right where he was. Scott would walk over and look through the glass and probably see him. Mike the meat man would walk around from the back and *definitely* see him.

He was stuck.

For the first time in a long time, Stick Dog didn't know what to do.

Then something hit him in the head.

Chapter 20

LUCY HELPS OUT

It was a yellow rope.

It was the yellow rope that he had seen in that German shepherd's—Lucy's—mouth in the truck at the parking lot.

Stick Dog snapped his head around.

He saw her there.

His heart raced.

His heart fluttered.

Lucy leaped toward him.

She stopped right in front of him. She picked
up the rope with her mouth and pointed
urgently toward the door at the back of the
store.

Stick Dog understood.

Lucy was helping him.

He got down low and
scurried on his belly as fast as he could
toward that door. While he did that, Lucy
ran around the front of the case with
her rope. She
jumped and
yelped and
wagged her tail.

Scott, the customer, jumped back a bit and stared at her.

Mike the meat man came to a halt. He looked over the opposite glass case at her. He seemed surprised too.

"Lucy-girl!" he called happily. "What are you so excited about? You want to play? I thought you were taking a nap in the back room!"

Lucy jumped and barked and wagged her tail even more.

"All right, all right!" Mike said, and changed direction, coming out from behind the glass cases on the other side. Stick Dog saw this and hurried into the back room.

Inside the back room, Stick Dog saw a desk, a chair, a back door with a belt hanging on it, a blanket, several cardboard boxes, and two big silver refrigerators. He picked out the darkest corner of the room and backed into it. He listened to what happened out in the store.

He heard Mike the meat man play tug-of-war with Lucy for a minute. He heard the two male humans discuss the proper way to cook hamburgers on a grill. He heard Mike package up some hamburgers and hot dogs for Scott. He heard two more customers come in.

And then he heard Lucy pad her way toward the back room.

He watched the doorway.

He saw her come in—and he knew he had to trust her. He was trapped. And she had already helped him. He stepped from the darkness of the corner.

"I'm Stick Dog," he said. He felt the words catch in the back of his throat for a second, but managed to get them out. "Thanks for helping me."

"I'm Lucy," she said. "You're welcome."

Stick Dog lowered his head and stared at the floor. He didn't know what to say. He was confused. He had never felt flustered before. He had always been confident. And now he was nervous. A weird nervous. A kind of nervous he hadn't felt before.

"Where are your friends?" Lucy asked.

"My friends?" Stick Dog asked, lifting his head.

"Yes," Lucy answered. "I saw them in the woods past the parking lot when we pulled away in the truck. When I was looking for you."

"You were, umm, looking for me?"

"I guess I was," Lucy answered slowly. Now it was her turn to look at the floor. She shuffled her front paws a little as she spoke.

"Sort of. Kind of. Umm. Yeah."

It was quiet then.

Like, awkward quiet.

But just for a moment.

Because right then something smashed into the back door.

Chapter 21

WHO ARE YOU?

Thump!

"What was that?" Lucy asked, breaking the silence and snapping her head around to look at the back door.

"Umm, I think I know," Stick Dog said. He had heard that noise many, many times before. "It's one of my friends. The poodle."

THUMP!

"What's he doing?"

"He's, umm, banging his head into the door."

"On purpose?!"

"Yes," he said, and nodded. After all these years, Poo-Poo bashing his head into things was completely normal to Stick Dog. But he realized that it wouldn't be normal to someone else. "It's just something he does. He's really, umm, good at it."

"That's an interesting skill," Lucy said.

"He's an interesting dog," Stick Dog said, and smiled. "Is there a way to open the door? I'd rather he doesn't keep banging into it. And am I safe back here? From your roommate?"

"You're safe," Lucy answered confidently and calmly. "Mike never comes back here while the store is open. He has to be out there for customers. And I can open the door. It's easy."

"It is?" Stick Dog answered. He had only seen humans open doors before.

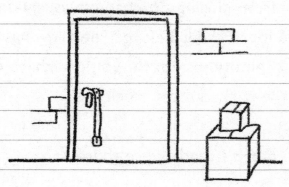

"Sure," Lucy said, and went to the door. She bit down on the belt that hung from the handle and pulled down on it. Then Lucy backed up with the belt in her mouth and opened the door. "I invented that. Mike, my human, was happy when I showed him. This way I can let myself out whenever I want."

Stick Dog was impressed.

They stepped outside to the alley behind Mike's Magnificent Meats. Lucy pushed a brick against the doorframe to keep the door from closing. She had obviously done this a lot of times before. The alley was totally empty except for some garbage cans and the parked meat truck.

Stick Dog's friends were there too.

Stripes, Mutt, and Karen stared suspiciously at Lucy. Poo-Poo did not. He was there, but his eyes were closed, and he was rubbing his head.

"Poo-Poo, did you bash into the door?" asked Stick Dog.

"Yeah, that was me," Poo-Poo answered simply, eyes still closed. "We thought you might be in there, so I tried to bash the door open."

"How's your head?" Lucy asked Poo-Poo.

"It's starting to feel really great," Poo-Poo replied. He kept his eyes shut and continued to rub his head. "It was aching and

throbbing for a minute, but now I'm getting that awesome numb-y feeling. I love it when that terrible hurt feeling goes away—it makes the initial pain totally worth it."

"So, you hurt yourself on purpose, and then you like the way it feels when the pain goes away?" Lucy asked. She obviously thought the whole idea was pretty absurd. "Couldn't you, you know, just not hurt yourself at all?"

"Where's the logic in that?" Poo-Poo asked, and then opened his eyes. "Hey, wait a minute. Who are you?"

"I'm Lucy."

"Lucy just helped me inside the store," Stick Dog stepped forward and explained. "I was trapped and about to get caught, but she got me out of it."

When Stripes, Karen, Mutt, and Poo-Poo heard this, they cast away their suspicions and doubt about Lucy. Stick Dog took a minute to introduce everybody and then got back to the main subject.

"We tracked down the store from the information on the side of the truck," Stick Dog explained to Lucy. "We wanted to get some meat."

"You're hungry?" Lucy asked.

"We're always hungry," Mutt said.

"Don't your humans feed you?"

"We're strays," Stick Dog explained. "We

don't have any humans."

This fact seemed to surprise Lucy.

"Hey, Lucy?" Karen asked. It seemed like
she had something important to say.

"Yes?"

"Guess
what?"

"What?"

"I totally just dug, like, the deepest hole
ever!"

"Wow," Lucy said, and smiled.

"I'm a really good digger!"

"I bet you are."

Stick Dog listened and liked the way Lucy reacted to Karen. And he watched as she interacted with the other members of his gang.

"Then Karen got stuck," Stripes said, continuing the story. "At the bottom of the hole. She dug it so deep that she couldn't get out."

"I'm an excellent digger," Karen reiterated.

"You must be."

"So, we had to figure out a way to get her out of the hole," Mutt said. You could tell that thinking back on Karen being trapped in the hole made him a little nervous. He shook an old gardening glove out of his fur and began to chew on it.

Lucy noticed.

"Can you store things in your fur? And then shake them out whenever you want?"

Mutt nodded—and chewed.

"That's fantastic."

Mutt smiled—and chewed.

"So we had to rescue Karen from that deep hole," Poo-Poo explained.

Karen said, "I might be, like, the best digger in the whole world."

"That wouldn't surprise me at all," Lucy said to Karen, and then turned back to Poo-Poo. "So how did you rescue her?"

"Well, we had a bunch of good plans," Poo-Poo said for the group. He was sort of bragging a little bit. "We were going to go to the circus and get some balloons and get her out that way. Then we thought we'd fill the hole with drool and let her float to the top. Then we figured we could go to the opposite side of the Earth and dig upward to get her out."

"I see," Lucy said. She glanced sideways at Stick Dog and then back at Poo-Poo, Mutt, Stripes, and Karen. "Such clever ideas."

"I know, right?" said Stripes.

Lucy asked, "So, how did you finally get Karen, the super-awesome digger, out of the hole?"

"I don't even remember," Poo-Poo said, and lifted his head to think. The others didn't seem to remember either. "It had something to do with Stick Dog, I think."

"Yeah, I think he played a small role somehow," Karen added.

"Then guess what happened after we got Karen out?!" Stripes exclaimed, and giggled a little bit.

"What?"

"Stick Dog fell into the exact same hole!" Stripes yelped, and laughed. Mutt, Karen, and Poo-Poo laughed too. "He's so silly!"

Lucy looked at Stick Dog. He looked back at her and squeezed his lips together. He smiled and nodded. And Lucy seemed to somehow understand exactly what his expression meant.

"Hey, Lucy!"

"Yes, Karen."

"Can I ask you something?"

"Of course."

"Do you know what coffee is?!"

Before Lucy could answer, Stick Dog politely reentered the conversation.

"Karen, could you talk with Lucy about coffee later?" he asked. "I really want to see if there's a way for us to get something to eat."

"Sure, Stick Dog. No problem," Karen

replied. "While you're doing that, I think I'll just hop up and down for a while. I'm feeling really energetic!"

"Umm, okay," he answered slowly. He whispered to Lucy, "She had a lot of coffee earlier."

Karen asked, "What did you say, Stick Dog?"

"Nothing, nothing."

Then Karen began to hop up and down.

Lucy watched with amusement as Karen hopped. Lucy turned to Stick Dog and said, "You came here to try to get something to eat? From the store?"

"Yes."

"I can help you," Lucy said.

"I wasn't sure if you'd want to," Stick Dog said honestly. "I mean, it sort of seems like we'd be taking from *you*. And that doesn't feel right."

"Don't worry about it," Lucy answered. "I mean, you saw how much meat was in there, right? There's plenty. Besides, if you're hungry, you have to eat. No matter what."

Stick Dog nodded.

"Let's go inside," Lucy said, and pointed

toward the back door. "I've got an idea."

Stick Dog nodded again. Then he said to his friends, "You guys stay here. Just hide if anybody comes."

Chapter 22

OBVIOUSLY SMART

When they got to the back room of Mike's Magnificent Meats, Lucy got her yellow rope and dropped it on the floor.

"I'll use this," Lucy said.

"Okay," Stick Dog replied. "Are you going to play tug-of-war with your human like before?"

"No," Lucy said. "If I do that, he'll be standing. That would make it easier for him to see you through the glass case when you reach up to grab something. I'm going to get him to crouch down for a while. That way he can't see you."

"How are you going to do that?"

"Don't worry about it. I'm on it," Lucy answered, and turned her head toward the doorway to the store to listen.

"Okay," Stick Dog answered.

It was a strange feeling—a very strange feeling—for Stick Dog. He had always had to devise every plan, manage his friends, and study each detail for every food-snatching adventure.

And now he didn't.

He felt totally confident in Lucy. She was obviously smart.

"All right," Lucy said, turning back. "There are no customers. You just peek out the door, and when you see my human stoop down, that's when you can come out and grab something. You'll have less than a minute. Okay?"

"Okay."

"One more thing," Lucy said. "If you hear me whining or something, don't worry about it. I'm just acting."

"Okay," Stick Dog said again.

"Good luck," Lucy said. She gave Stick Dog a quick wink and hustled out to the store with the yellow rope.

And Stick Dog's heart
did that weird fluttering
thing again.

Chapter 23

WORKING TOGETHER

Stick Dog peeked out from the edge of
the doorway. He could see Mike the meat
man behind the counter. He was cutting
something with that big rectangular knife
again. Lucy walked right behind him and
around the corner of the glass case on
the farthest side of the store. Stick Dog

couldn't see her any longer. He could only see her human.

Mike the meat man must have heard Lucy pad behind him.

"How are you doing, Lucy-girl?" he asked without looking.

Lucy barked a friendly bark.

"Glad to hear it," he said, and chuckled a bit.

Stick Dog waited. He didn't know what Lucy was going to do. He just knew that when Mike the meat man crouched down, he'd need to move fast. He knew exactly what he was going to try to snatch.

Stick Dog waited.

Mike the meat man slammed that huge knife into something.

Whack!

WHACK!

Stick Dog waited.

WHACK!

Whack!

Stick Dog waited.

WHACK!

Whack!

Stick Dog waited.

And then Lucy started to whimper. It was a soft and pitiful sound. It sounded so sad.

WHIMPER...

Mike the meat man put that giant knife down
and turned around. He wiped his hands on
his apron.

"What is it, Lucy-
girl?" he called.
He walked toward
where Lucy was—
and turned the corner where Lucy had
disappeared behind the glass case.

Stick Dog couldn't see Lucy, of course. But
he could see Mike the meat man.

"What is it?" Mike repeated.

Lucy whined some more.

"Is there something under there, Lucy-girl?
Did you lose something?" he asked.

And then he crouched down.

Stick Dog moved—and moved fast. As he listened to what was happening, he hustled to the nearest glass case and propped himself up. He saw what he was after.

Lucy whined.

"How in the world did your rope get under this case?!" Mike the meat man said. "That's why you're upset. Your favorite thing is out of reach. Poor thing. I'll get it for you. It's really far back there."

As Mike the meat man grunted, groaned, and stretched to reach the rope that Lucy had deliberately pushed under the case, Stick Dog reached for the foot-long hot dogs with his mouth.

He grabbed as many as he could, ducked his head out of the case, and dropped quietly back to all fours. He padded softly and quickly toward the back room. He tucked himself back into that dark corner, dropping the hot dogs at his paws.

Lucy yelped a happy bark.

"There you go, Lucy-girl!" Mike the meat man said. "Run along now. I need to get back to work."

Lucy barked again.

"You're welcome."

Stick Dog smiled.

He could hear Lucy
coming back.

Chapter 24

WHY WERE YOU HIDING?

When Lucy returned, she dropped the rope on the floor and came directly toward Stick Dog. She looked down at his front paws.

"You chose the foot-long hot dogs," she observed. "Good thinking. That's what I would have grabbed too."

Stick Dog nodded, appreciating her praise.

"That was a good idea with the rope," he said to Lucy. "You're a really good actress."

Lucy nodded, appreciating his praise.

They took no time getting back outside. Lucy opened the door, Stick Dog picked up the foot-long hot dogs, and they went to find their friends. They knew the other dogs were hungry. After Lucy pushed the brick into place to keep the back door open, they looked around.

But only Karen was there.

"Hi, Karen," Stick Dog said after dropping the foot-long hot dogs. "Where's everybody else?"

"I don't know," Karen said and shrugged. "They were here a minute ago."

"Here we are," Stripes said, coming out from behind a garbage can. Poo-Poo and Mutt came out too.

"Why were you hiding?" Lucy asked.

"Well, Karen ran down the alley a little ways," Poo-Poo began to explain as they all came closer. He appeared to be speaking for Mutt and Stripes as well.

"I got tired of jumping," Karen said. "I jumped, like, a million times. And it got boring after a while. But I still felt super-energetic. So I decided to run down the alley and then come back."

"Right, she got tired of jumping," Poo-Poo said. "She ran down there—and then she came back."

"Okay," Stick Dog said slowly. "But, umm, why were you hiding?"

"Because Karen came back," Poo-Poo said. "That's why."

Lucy was as confused as Stick Dog. She repeated his question, "But why were you hiding?"

"Because Stick Dog said to hide if anybody comes," Poo-Poo explained further. "Karen came. So we hid."

"But you *know* Karen," Stick Dog stated. "You don't need to hide from Karen."

"You said *anybody*, Stick Dog," Mutt stated. He wanted to help them understand. "That's a direct quote."

"Are you saying Karen's not anybody?" Stripes asked, trying to prove their point. "I mean, that's kind of a rude thing to say."

Lucy looked at Stick Dog. Stick Dog looked at Lucy. They both grinned very slightly at one another. The other dogs did not see this.

"That's not what I'm saying," Stick Dog said. "I understand why you were hiding now. Thanks for explaining it to us."

Then Lucy pointed at the foot-long hot dogs and said, "Look what we got."

And Mutt, Karen, Stripes, and Poo-Poo started to drool.

Chapter 25

YIKES

Stick Dog had grabbed as many of the
foot-long hot dogs as he could. He hadn't
counted them. There wasn't enough time,
and they were all tangled up
anyway. But now that it
was time to eat, he
realized there were only
five meaty treats.

Poo-Poo took one.

Karen took one.

Stripes took one.

And Mutt took one.

There was one foot-long hot dog left.

"You eat it," Lucy offered. "You're hungrier than me."

"No, I'm fine," Stick Dog said, and shook his head politely. "It was your plan. You should eat it."

"Share?" Lucy asked.

"Share," Stick Dog agreed.

Lucy started eating the foot-long hot dog from one end.

Stick Dog started eating the foot-long hot dog from the other end.

Then they met in the middle.

(Yikes.)

Chapter 26

ROMANTICAL?

While the other dogs finished eating, Lucy
and Stick Dog chatted for a moment. They
didn't have much time to talk—Mutt,
Karen, Stripes, and Poo-Poo finished their
hot dogs quickly. They gathered around
Stick Dog and Lucy after making sure there
wasn't a single nibble left.

"Those hot dogs were
gigantic," Stripes said with
satisfaction as she rubbed her
belly.

Poo-Poo added, "And delicious."

Mutt licked his lips as he smiled and agreed.

Karen chased her tail.

"What were you two talking about?" Poo-Poo asked.

"I was telling Stick Dog that it's time for me to head back inside," Lucy said. "The store is about to close, and my human will be looking for me."

"And it's about time we got back to my pipe," Stick Dog said. "It's been a long day."

"But what about Lucy?" Karen asked as she spun slowly to a stop. "Is she coming with us?"

"No, she's staying here with her human," Stick Dog explained. "She has him pretty well-trained. And she likes it here."

"What's not to like?" Poo-Poo asked. He understood. "I mean, a store full of meat. She can come and go whenever she wants. It's not too bad at all."

Lucy smiled at this.

"I want to see you again," she said, and looked directly back at Stick Dog. Then, turning to the others, she added, "I mean, I want to see all of you again."

"We're going to come back here to visit," Stick Dog said, and looked directly at Lucy.

Karen noticed how Lucy and Stick Dog

stared at each other for a second.

"Wait a minute," she said. "You two are acting weird. What's going on?"

Stick Dog and Lucy didn't answer.

Karen squinted one eye and tilted her head. She asked, "Is this one of those romantical situations?"

Stripes said, "Gross."

Mutt said, "Strange."

Poo-Poo said, "Hunh?"

And Stick Dog just said, "Come on. It's time to go."

And they went.

Chapter 27

K-I-S-S-I-N-G!

They got back to Stick Dog's pipe, and their conversation continued.

"Stick Dog and Lucy sitting in a tree," Stripes said in a sing-songy rhythm. *"K-I-S-S-I-N-G!"*

This caught Poo-Poo's attention.

"Stick Dog?" he asked suddenly. "Do you know how to climb trees?! Stripes just mentioned it. If you do, could you teach me?"

"Umm—" he tried to answer, but Poo-Poo interrupted him.

"If you taught me how to climb trees, I could take care of the menacing squirrel population around here in minutes," Poo-Poo assured. "Why, you wouldn't see one of those chittering, puffy-tailed villains for miles!"

"I don't know how to climb a tree," Stick Dog said calmly. He was in a very good mood. His friends were fed. And he thought they might go back to see Lucy in the next few days.

"Sooooo," Karen asked, stretching the word out. "When you and Lucy were talking, was it romantical?"

"Yeah, Stick Dog," Stripes chimed in. "Is this romantical? I mean, are you, like, Lucy's 'Stick Dude' now? And is she, like, your 'Stick Chick'?"

Stick Dog didn't even think "romantical" was a word, so he didn't feel at all dishonest when he said, "We were not talking about anything romantical."

"Then what were you talking about?" Karen persisted.

"Well, one thing we talked about was that there are some days when we can't find anything to eat," Stick Dog explained. "And Lucy said that on those days, we could always come back to see her, and we could get something at the meat store. We won't stop searching for food and going on adventures, of course. But if there's ever a time when we can't find anything, then we can go see Lucy and get something there."

This was an absolutely shocking idea to Mutt, Stripes, Karen, and Poo-Poo. They had, after all, spent every day of the past few years hunting for things to fill their bellies.

"So, let me get this straight," Poo-Poo said. It didn't sound like he couldn't *understand* what he just heard. It was more like he couldn't *believe* what he just heard. "You mean, we never have to worry about being hungry again? We can go to sleep and know that—no matter what—we will have something to eat the next day? Because we can always go see Lucy?"

"That's exactly what I mean," Stick Dog said.

"That's totally awesome!" Karen exclaimed, speaking for the group.

Stick Dog smiled a bit to himself. He was looking forward to seeing Lucy again. And he was looking forward to all the days ahead with his friends.

They would continue their food hunts together. They'd often be successful. But whenever they weren't, they would always have something to eat.

Always.

And that was a good—a really good—
feeling.

"You're right," Stick Dog said, and smiled at
his friends. "It is awesome."

THE END.

Tom Watson lives in Chicago with his wife, daughter, and son. He also has a dog, as you could probably guess. The dog is a Labrador-Newfoundland mix. Tom says he looks like a Labrador with a bad perm. He wanted to name the dog "Put Your Shirt On" (please don't ask why), but he was outvoted by his family. The dog's name is Shadow. Early in his career Tom worked in politics, including a stint as the chief speechwriter for the governor of Ohio. This experience helped him develop the unique storytelling narrative style of the Stick Dog, Stick Cat, and Trouble at Table 5 books. Tom's time in politics also made him realize a very important thing: kids are way smarter than adults. And it's a lot more fun and rewarding to write stories for them than to write speeches for grown-ups.

Visit www.stickdogbooks.com

for more fun stuff.

Also available as an ebook.